# THIS IS NOT A UNICORN!

For the boys at The Vintage Scoop, Fulham, whose perfect falafel wraps helped me write this story on Friday lunchtimes – B. T.

To Chris F, a real-life unicorn – G.A.

First published 2021 by Nosy Crow Ltd
The Crow's Nest, 14 Baden Place, Crosby Row, London SE1 1YW
www.nosycrow.com

ISBN 978 1 83994 287 7 (HB)
ISBN 978 1 83994 288 4 (PB)



A CIP catalogue record for this book is available from the British Library.

Printed in Italy
Papers used by Nosy Crow are made from wood grown in sustainable forests.

1 3 5 7 9 8 6 4 2 (HB)
1 3 5 7 9 8 6 4 2 (PB)

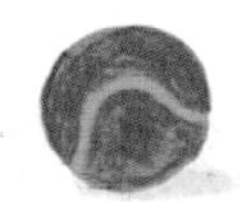

# THIS IS NOT A UNICORN!

BARRY TIMMS

GED ADAMSON

Hey there, you!
Step right this way.
You're in for such a treat!
For there's a special animal
I think you'd like to meet . . .

The thing that makes it special
is its sparkling magic horn.
But do not be mistaken . . .

this is **NOT** a unicorn.

It's a . . .

. . . tune-icorn.
A spoon-icorn.

A blow-up-your-balloon-icorn.

A make-a-secret-wish-icorn.

A catch-the-biggest-fish-icorn!

This creature's never what it seems.
You might be feeling torn,
but let's make one thing very clear –

it's **NOT** a unicorn!

It's a . . .

. . . pour-icorn.

An oar-icorn.

An open-up-the-door-icorn.

A tickly-under-there-icorn.

A hover-in-the-air-icorn!

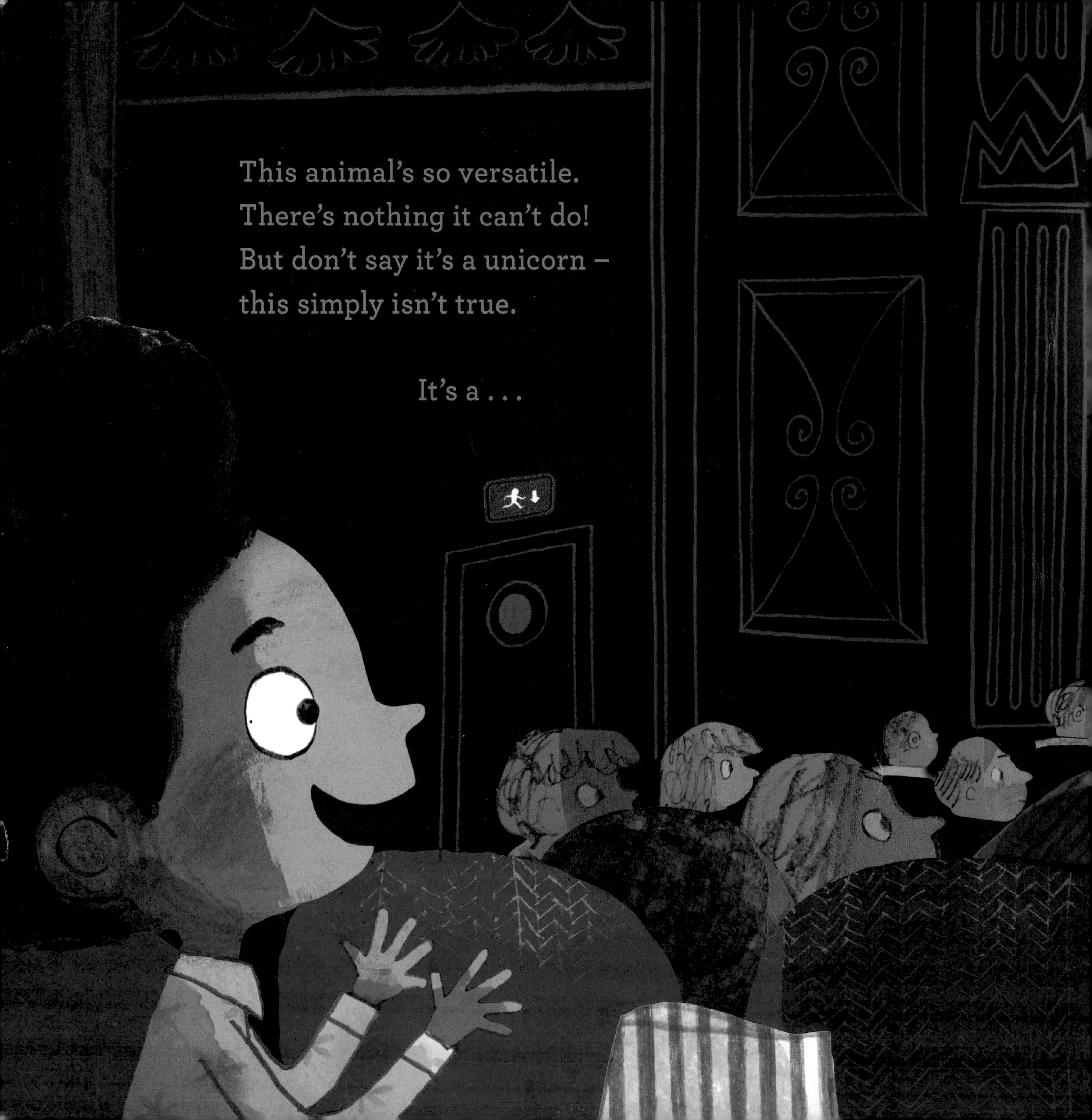

This animal's so versatile.
There's nothing it can't do!
But don't say it's a unicorn –
this simply isn't true.

It's a . . .

NOT
A
UNICORN!

. . . skip-icorn.

A snip-icorn.

A triple-pancake flip-icorn.
Today's Menu
A hurry-up-and-play-icorn.

A lamp-to-light-your-way-icorn.

A singing-in-the-rain-icorn.

A look-inside-
your-brain-icorn.

A make-your-garden-
bloom-icorn.

I CORN 1

# A rocket-to-the-moon-icorn!

Wow! What a clever animal.
So many things in one!

We need a name that stands for
all these different kinds of fun.

Think-icorn . . .

think-icorn . . .

shhh, don't-even-blink-icorn . . .

Suddenly-it's-clear-icorn!
Whisper-in-your-ear-icorn.

The animal has spoken,
and at last I can report –

it's the perfect-friend-for-you-nicorn.

Or . . .

. . . just 'you-nicorn' for short!